ISSUE #5

JURASSIC SENTRIES

" MUTATIONS "

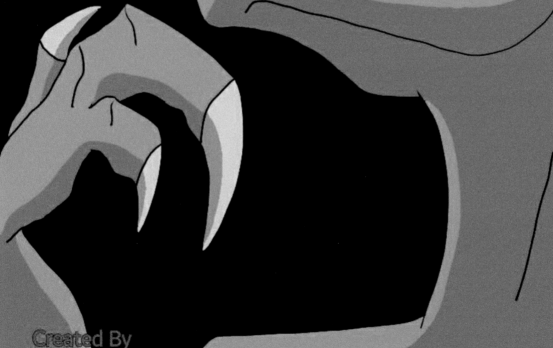

Created By
DEION TILLETT

To order additional copies of this book, contact:
Xlibris
844-714-8691
www.Xlibris.com
Orders@Xlibris.com

ISBN: Softcover   978-1-6641-9641-4
        EBook   978-1-6641-9642-1

Print information available on the last page

Rev. date: 10/22/2021

PREVIOUSLY ON JURASSIC SENTRIES

Finally after Rex has healed from his injury, the Sentries received a message from a Dr. Korrosave. A genetics engineer planning to clone Saurian DNA and build an army to replace the Sentries. In order to stop him the team rush to his location before he can release these creatures onto the city. However, the Sentries fell into a hidden trap, what creatures will they have to face?

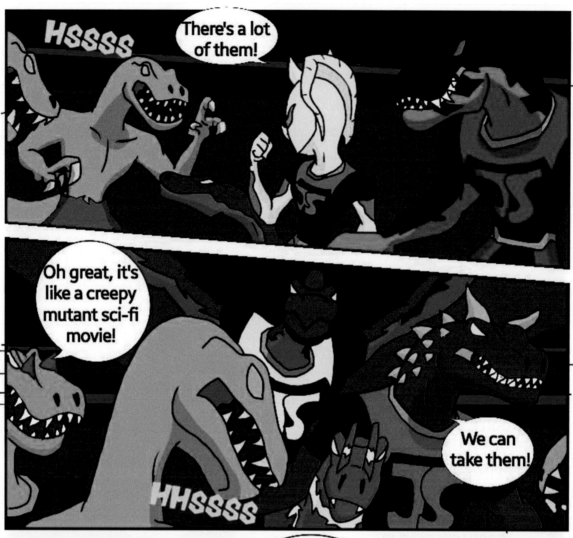

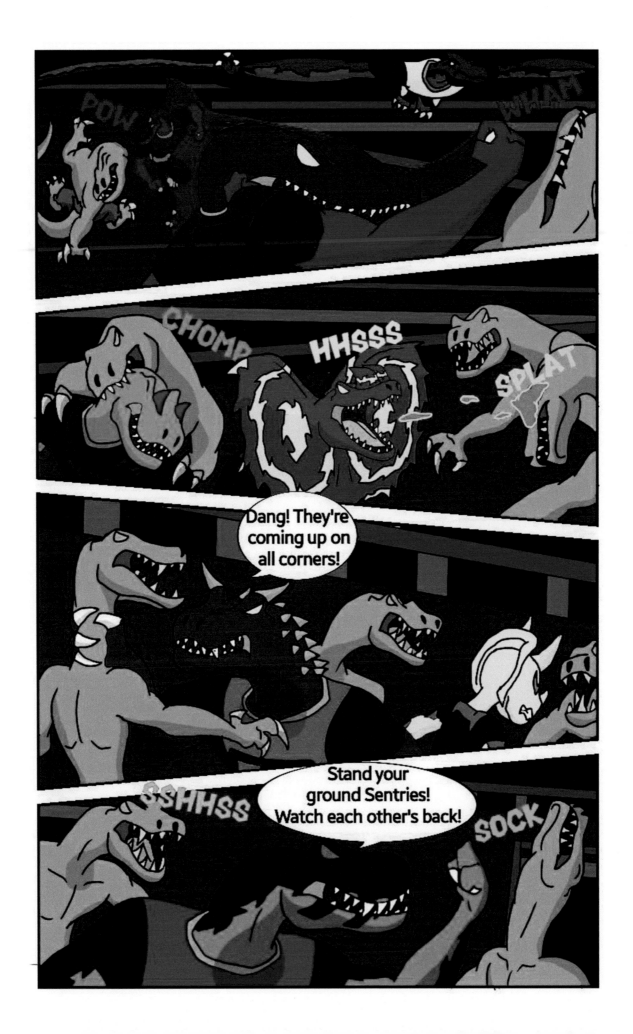

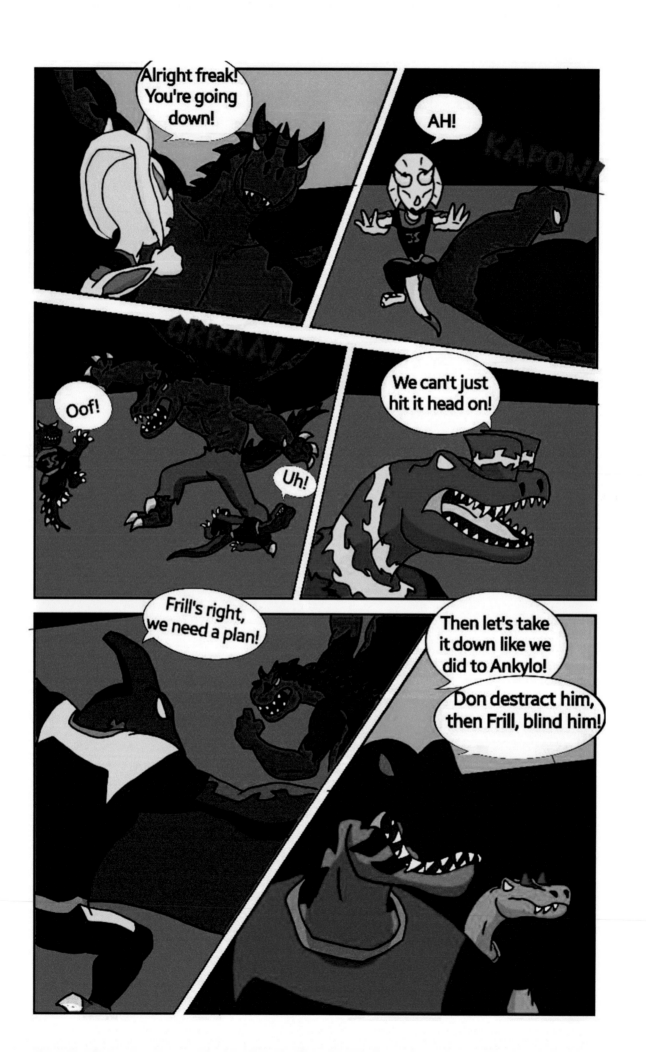

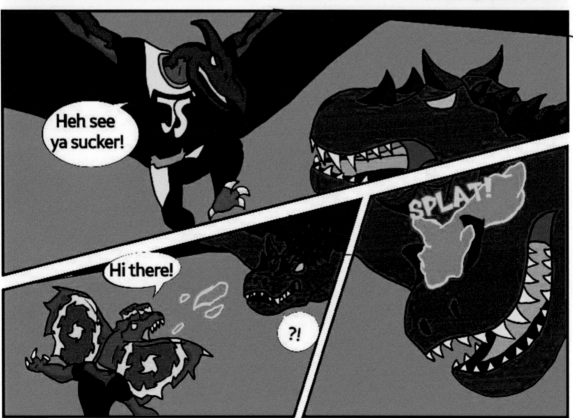

JURASSIC SENTRIES

ISSUE #6

NEXT ISSUE : " ANTI-REX"

Created By
DEION TILLETT